This beach journal belongs to:

hermit crab

Date: _____

Weather: ☀ ☁ 🌧 ⛈ 🌬

my beach journal

Beach visited:_____

My favorite thing about the day:_____

_____

The coolest thing I saw . . . _____

_____

Draw or write about your day at the beach!

Would you rather be a
dolphin or a shark?

Date: _____

Weather: ☀ ☁ 🌧 ⛈ 🌬

my beach journal

Beach visited:_____

My favorite thing about the day:_____

_____

The coolest thing I saw . . . _____

_____

Draw or write about your day at the beach!

Date: _____

Weather: ☀ ☁ 🌧 ⛈ 🌬

my beach journal

each visited:_____

y favorite thing about the day:_____

_____

ie coolest thing I saw . . . _____

_____

Draw or write about your day at the beach!

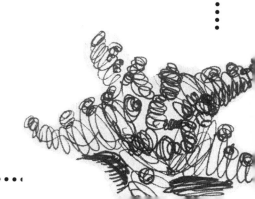

Date: _____

Weather: ☀ ☁ 🌧 ⛈ 🌬

my beach journal

Beach visited:_____

My favorite thing about the day:_____

_____

The coolest thing I saw . . . _____

_____

Draw or write about your day at the beach!

Shells shells shells!

- trace shells
- Place shells under paper and rub over the top with crayon to see the texture
- Put shells in a small baggie and staple to this page
- Important: make sure you don't take any shells that are alive (like live sea stars or sand dollars) or shells that have critters living in them. Ask an adult if you aren't sure!

Date: _____

Weather: ☀ ☁ 🌧 ⛈ 🌬

my beach journal

Beach visited:_____

My favorite thing about the day:_____

_____

The coolest thing I saw . . . _____

_____

Draw or write about your day at the beach!

Huge waves: fun or
FREAKY?!

Date: _____

Weather: ☀ ☁ 🌧 ⛈ 🌬

my beach journal

Beach visited:_____

My favorite thing about the day:_____

_____

The coolest thing I saw . . . _____

_____

Draw or write about your day at the beach!

Date: _____

Weather: ☀ ☁ 🌧 ⛈ 🌬

my beach journal

each visited:_____

y favorite thing about the day:_____

_____

e coolest thing I saw . . . _____

_____

Draw or write about your day at the beach!

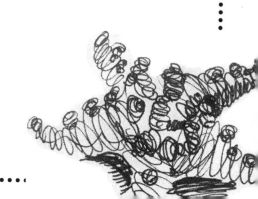

Date: _____

Weather: ☀ ☁ 🌧 ⛈ 🌬

my beach journal

Beach visited:_____

My favorite thing about the day:_____

_____

The coolest thing I saw . . . _____

_____

Draw or write about your day at the beach!

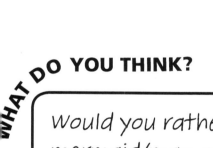

Would you rather be a mermaid/man or pirate?

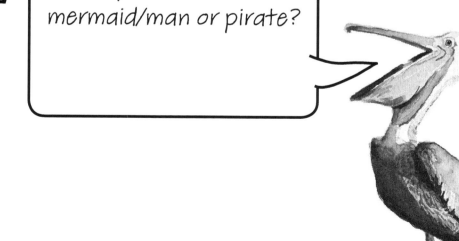

Date: _____

Weather: ☀ ☁ 🌧 ⛈ 🌬

my beach journal

Beach visited:_____

My favorite thing about the day:_____

_____

The coolest thing I saw . . . _____

_____

Draw or write about your day at the beach!

Date: _____

Weather: ☀ ☁ 🌧 ⛈ 💨

my beach journal

each visited:_____

y favorite thing about the day:_____

_____

ie coolest thing I saw . . . _____

_____

Draw or write about your day at the beach!

Date: _____

Weather: ☀ ☁ 🌧 ⛈ 💨

my beach journal

Beach visited:_____

My favorite thing about the day:_____

_____

The coolest thing I saw . . . _____

_____

Draw or write about your day at the beach!

horseshoe crab

KOOKY for CRABS!

hermit crab

hermit crab

sand fiddler

Crabs I have seen:

- ☐ ghost crab
- ☐ hermit crab
- ☐ horseshoe crab
- ☐ sand-fiddler crab

I run sideways and backwards like a crustacean ninja!

ghost crab

Date: _____

Weather: ☀ ☁ 🌧 ⛈ 🌬

my beach journal

Beach visited:_____

My favorite thing about the day:_____

_____

The coolest thing I saw . . . _____

_____

Draw or write about your day at the beach!

What would you do if you found hidden treasure at the beach?

Date: _____

Weather: ☀ ☁ 🌧 ⛈ 🌬

my beach journal

Beach visited:_____

My favorite thing about the day:_____

_____

The coolest thing I saw . . . _____

_____

Draw or write about your day at the beach!

Date: _____

Weather: ☀ ☁ 🌧 ⛈ 💨

my beach journal

ach visited:_____

y favorite thing about the day:_____

_____

ie coolest thing I saw . . . _____

_____

Draw or write about your day at the beach!

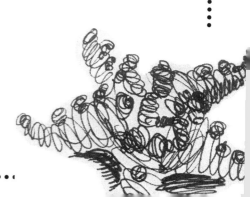

Date: _____

Weather: ☀ ☁ 🌧 ⛈ 🌬

my beach journal

Beach visited:_____

My favorite thing about the day:_____

_____

The coolest thing I saw . . . _____

_____

Draw or write about your day at the beach!

Would you rather go sailing or surfing?

Date: _____

Weather: ☀ ☁ ☔ ⛈ 🌬

my beach journa.

Beach visited:_____

My favorite thing about the day:_____

_____

The coolest thing I saw . . . _____

_____

Draw or write about your day at the beach!

Date: _____

Weather: ☀ ☁ 🌧 ⛈ 💨

my beach journal

ach visited:_____

y favorite thing about the day:_____

_____

e coolest thing I saw . . . _____

_____

Draw or write about your day at the beach!

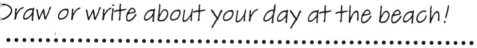

Have you seen

sea creatures I've seen:

- ☐ dolphin
- ☐ jellyfish
- ☐ fish
- ☐ shark
- ☐ sea turtle
- ☐ sting ray
- ☐ crabs
- ☐ mermaids

sea creatures?

Date: _____

Weather: ☀ ☁ 🌧 ⛈ 🌬

my beach journa

Beach visited:_____

My favorite thing about the day:_____

_____

The coolest thing I saw . . . _____

_____

Draw or write about your day at the beach!

Draw your favorite shell!

Date: _____

Weather: ☀ ☁ 🌧 ⛈ 🌬

my beach journal

Beach visited:_____

My favorite thing about the day:_____

_____

The coolest thing I saw . . . _____

_____

Draw or write about your day at the beach!

Date: _____

Weather: ☀ ☁ 🌧 ⛈ 🌬

my beach journal

ach visited:_____

y favorite thing about the day:_____

_____

e coolest thing I saw . . . _____

_____

Draw or write about your day at the beach!

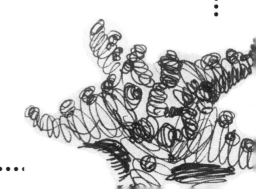

Date: _____

Weather: ☀ ☁ 🌧 ⛈ 🌬

my beach journa

Beach visited:_____

My favorite thing about the day:_____

_____

The coolest thing I saw . . . _____

_____

Draw or write about your day at the beach!

WHAT DO YOU THINK?

What's your pirate name?

Date: _____

Weather: ☀ ☁ 🌧 ⛈ 💨

my beach journa

Beach visited:_____

My favorite thing about the day:_____

_____

The coolest thing I saw . . . _____

_____

Draw or write about your day at the beach!

Date: _____

Weather: ☀ ☁ 🌧 ⛈ 💨

my beach journal

ach visited:_____

favorite thing about the day:_____

_____

coolest thing I saw . . . _____

_____

Draw or write about your day at the beach!

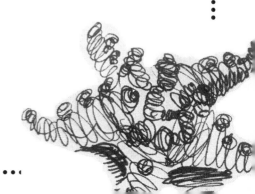

SQUAWK SQUAWK!

Have you spotted an of these birds?

Shorebirds I've seen:

☐ plover

☐ sand piper

☐ royal tern

☐ egret

☐ Oystercatcher

☐ Dowitcher

☐ gull

☐ sanderling

☐ _____

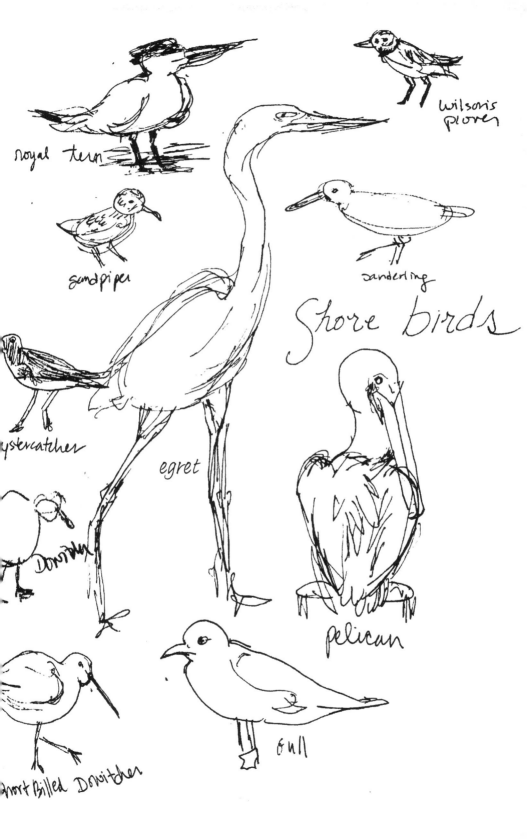

royal tern

wilson's plover

sandpiper

sanderling

Shore birds

ystercatcher

egret

Dowitcher

pelican

hort Billed Dowitcher

gull

Date: _____

Weather: ☀ ☁ 🌧 ⛈ 🌬

my beach journal

Beach visited:_____

My favorite thing about the day:_____
_____

The coolest thing I saw . . . _____
_____

Draw or write about your day at the beach!

WHAT DO YOU THINK?

Would you rather live on land or sea?

Date: _____

Weather: ☀ ☁ 🌧 ⛈ 🌬

my beach journa

Beach visited:_____

My favorite thing about the day:_____

_____

The coolest thing I saw . . . _____

_____

Draw or write about your day at the beach!

Date: _____

Weather: ☀ ☁ 🌧 ⛈ 🌬

my beach journal

ach visited:_____

y favorite thing about the day:_____

_____

e coolest thing I saw . . . _____

_____

Draw or write about your day at the beach!

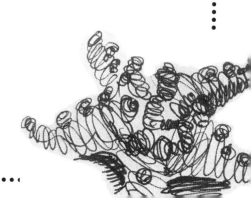

Date: _____

Weather: ☼ ☁ ☔ ⛈ 🌬

my beach journa

Beach visited:_____

My favorite thing about the day:_____

_____

The coolest thing I saw . . . _____

_____

Draw or write about your day at the beach!

WHAT DO YOU THINK?

Coolest shark: great white or hammerhead?

Date: _____

Weather: ☀ ☁ 🌧 ⛈ 🌬

my beach journal

Beach visited:_____

My favorite thing about the day:_____

_____

The coolest thing I saw . . . _____

_____

Draw or write about your day at the beach!

Date: _____

Weather: ☼ ☁ 🌧 ⛈ 🌬

my beach journal

each visited:_____

y favorite thing about the day:_____
_____

ie coolest thing I saw . . . _____
_____

Draw or write about your day at the beach!

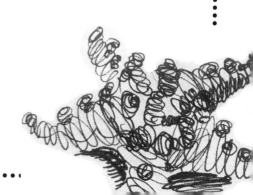

Date: _____

Weather: ☀ ☁ ☔ ⛈ 🌬

my beach journa

Beach visited:_____

My favorite thing about the day:_____

_____

The coolest thing I saw . . . _____

_____

Draw or write about your day at the beach!

WHAT DO YOU THINK?

Pelicans: great or GREATEST beach bird ever?!

58921923R00029

Made in the USA
Middletown, DE
08 August 2019